Lion Dancer

Ernie Wan's Chinese New Year

By Kate Waters and Madeline Slovenz-Low
Photographs by Martha Cooper

SCHOLASTIC INC. ◆ New York

To the Wan Chi Ming Hung Gar School
and to future generations of lion dancers.

Our warmest and sincere thanks to the Wan family—Mr. and Mrs. Wan, Jenny, Ernie, and Warren—who graciously allowed us to enter the privacy of their home and join them in their New Year celebrations; to Jimmy Low, whose passion for the Lion Dance tradition and his desire to convey that love is the foundation that made this book possible, for his generous contribution of time and patience in translating and communicating with the Wan family, the Wan Chi Ming Hung Gar School, and the New York Chinese School; to Chin Kwok Qui, the principal of the Chinese School, and Pu Que Yin, Ernie's Chinese teacher, for permitting us to observe and photograph during school hours; to Barbara Kirshenblatt-Gimblett, Chair of the Department of Performance Studies at NYU for leading the way; to City Lore, Inc.: the New York Center for Urban Folk Culture, where the photographs will be archived; to Grace How, photo researcher, who tracked down the photographs that led to this collaboration; to Phoebe Yeh, who acted as interpreter at our first meeting with the Wan family; and to Alvin Ho, age 7, the unsung hero who dances in the lion's tail. The source used for the Chinese Horoscope section is: Theodora Lau.
The Handbook of Chinese Horoscopes (revised edition), Perennial Library, Harper & Row Publishers, New York, 1988.

Library of Congress Cataloging-in-Publication Data available.
Library of Congress number: 89-6423
ISBN 0-590-43046-7

12 11 10 9 8 7 6 5 4 3   1 2 3 4 5/9
Printed in the U.S.A.   36
First Scholastic printing, February 1990

Hi! My name is Ernie Wan.

This is my father, my mother, my sister Jenny, and my little brother Warren.

We live in an apartment in Chinatown.

This is the story of the most important day in my life.

This Chinese New Year, I will perform my first Lion Dance on the streets of New York City.

This is Chinatown.

Every day on my way home from school, I see something different.

Greenmarket

Fish seller

Ice carver

Restaurant window

At Chinese New Year, thousands of visitors will come to watch our celebrations. Then we will have a hard time walking down the sidewalk.

Jenny and I go to public school during the week. But on Saturdays, we go to a special Chinese school where we learn to read and write in Chinese. Writing is the hardest!

Today it is very hard for me to sit still.
Chinese New Year starts tonight. And
tomorrow morning, I will dance in the street.

Finally school is finished. Jenny and I race to class at my father's kung fu school. We have been learning martial arts since we were three years old. Today we practice the Lion Dance. The dance will scare away evil spirits and bring good luck for the New Year.

After class, my father tells me to check my new lion's head.

I pull the strings inside that make its ears wiggle and its eyes blink.

Then I test the switch inside that makes its eyes light up.

My father watches me go through my dance one more time before we leave. On the way home, he tells me that I am doing well, and that my dance will bring honor to our family.

When we get home, my mother is waiting for us. She helps me put on my new clothes.

Jenny helps Warren with his. It is our custom to wear something brand-new for the New Year. That way, the evil spirits won't recognize us.

My mother has been cooking all day. She cooks in a pot called a wok.

When everything is done, she puts the food in front of the altar. The altar honors all of our family ancestors. Offering food and incense at the altar is a Buddhist tradition.

First we bow at the altar.

Now we can sit down to eat.

There are oysters, fishballs, shrimp, chicken, pork, seaweed, lotus root, and of course, rice. What a feast!

After dinner, my mother lets Warren and me play Lion Dance music.

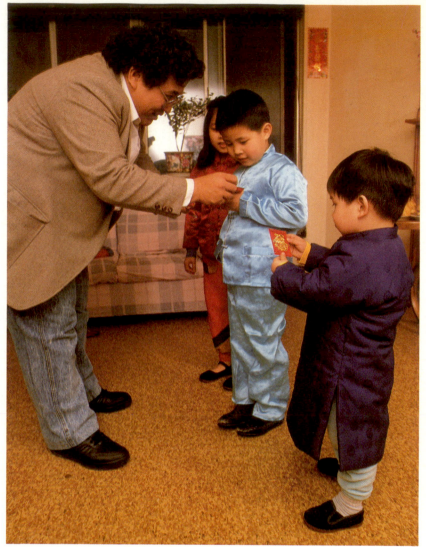

Later, Uncle Jimmy comes. *"Gung-Hey-Fat-Choy!"* we shout. That means Happy New Year. He gives us each a red envelope with money in it. We will get many more red envelopes for the New Year.

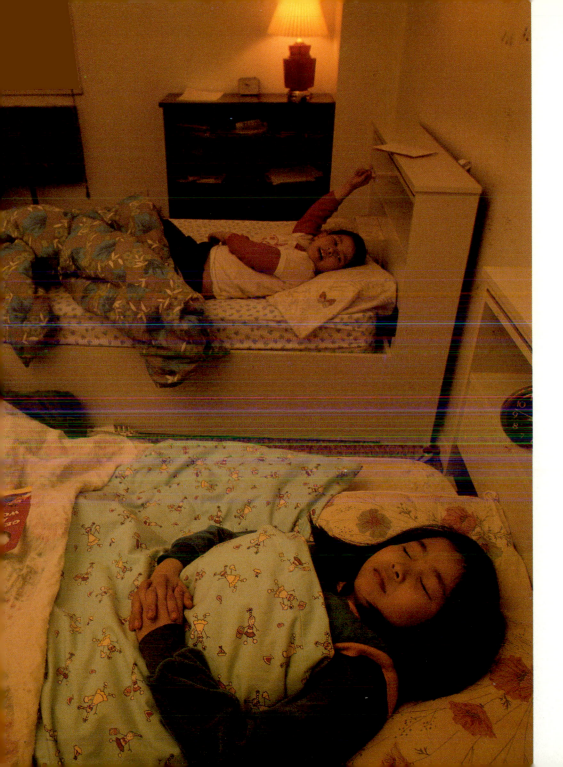

The eye-opening ceremony will begin at midnight. My mother sends Jenny and me to our room to take a nap. But I can't sleep.

At 11 o'clock, my father gets
us up. We walk back to his school.
It's fun to be up so late at night.
My father helps me, Jenny, and our
friend Alvin with our uniforms.

A few minutes before midnight, my father begins
the eye-opening ceremony for my lion.
All new lions have one.

He honors the school's ancestors.

He mixes red cinnabar and rice wine.
Red is good luck.

He dabs my lion's eyes, ears, nose,
mouth, and body with the red mixture.

Our dance begins. We must always keep the lion moving. I watch the other dancers to make sure I stay in step. Jenny and Alvin take turns dancing in the tail.

At the end of the dance, the Buddha leads us
right up to the firecrackers. Then...

...BANG! BANG! BANG! BANG! BANG! The room is full of noise and smoke!

The Lion Dance is done for tonight. Before we go home, we watch a videotape of the ceremony. We make sure we did our steps right. Tomorrow is the big day. We will dance in the streets!

We meet early the next morning. People outside are already beginning to shoot off firecrackers. My uncle gives me last-minute instructions.

We go up and down the streets. The lion must never stop moving.

We go inside restaurants and stores to bring good-luck
blessings. Every place we go, people give us red envelopes.

Outside, shopkeepers hang
long strings of firecrackers.

I stay back when the Buddha
leads the big lions close to the
firecrackers. Because of all the noise
and smoke, all the dancers must
cover their mouths and ears.

Down the street, a shopkeeper has made a
snake puzzle. He has hidden a red envelope
somewhere in the bowl. The dancers must find it.

The dancer in the lion's head hops up on the bowl. He grabs the
toy snakes and throws them into the crowd. Then he gobbles the
lettuce and spits it out. He finds the red envelope inside the lettuce!
Then, BANG! BANG! BANG! BANG! BANG! More firecrackers.

Finally it is time for me to dance in my neighborhood. My family, neighbors, and many visitors have come to watch.

When we finish,
everyone claps and cheers.

I am too tired to walk back to my father's school, so I hop on the drum cart and ride.
Gung-Hey-Fat-Choy!

The Chinese lunar calendar is 2,637 years older than ours. Each year is named for an animal. Every 12 years this cycle begins again. The Chinese say that the animal ruling the year you were born will influence your life. Beginning with the Rat, the wheel reads counterclockwise.

Chinese Horoscope

It is the Chinese custom to name each year after an animal.
Can you find the year you were born?

Year of the Rat

1948, 1960, 1972, 1984, 1996, 2008
Rat people are very popular. They like to invent things and are good artists.

Year of the Ox

1949, 1961, 1973, 1985, 1997, 2009
People born in this year are dependable and calm. They are good listeners and have very strong ideas.

Year of the Tiger

1950, 1962, 1974, 1986, 1998, 2010
Tiger people are brave. Other people respect tiger people for their deep thoughts and courageous actions.

Year of the Rabbit

1951, 1963, 1975, 1987, 1999, 2011
People born in this year are nice to be around. They like to talk, and many people trust them.

Year of the Dragon

1952, 1964, 1976, 1988, 2000, 2012
Dragon people have good health and lots of energy. They are good friends because they listen carefully to others.

Year of the Snake

1941, 1953, 1965, 1977, 1989, 2001
People born in this year love good books, food, music, and plays. They will have good luck with money.

Year of the Horse

1942, 1954, 1966, 1978, 1990, 2002
People born in this year are popular, cheerful, and are quick to compliment others. Horse people can work very hard.

Year of the Sheep

1943, 1955, 1967, 1979, 1991, 2003
People born in this year are very good artists. They ask many questions, like nice things, and are very wise.

Year of the Monkey

1944, 1956, 1968, 1980, 1992, 2004
Monkey people are very funny. They can always make people laugh. They are also very good at solving problems.

Year of the Rooster

1945, 1957, 1969, 1981, 1993, 2005
People born in this year are hard workers. They have many talents and think deep thoughts.

Year of the Dog

1946, 1958, 1970, 1982, 1994, 2006
Dog people are loyal and can always keep a secret. Sometimes dog people worry too much.

Year of the Boar

1947, 1959, 1971, 1983, 1995, 2007
People born in this year are very good students. They are honest and brave. They always finish a project or assignment.